ART SMART, SCIENCE DETECTIVE

Young
Palmetto
Books

Kim Shealy Jeffcoat, Series Editor

ART SMART
SCIENCE DETECTIVE

THE CASE OF THE SLIDING SPACESHIP

MELINDA LONG

ILLUSTRATED BY MONICA WYRICK

THE UNIVERSITY OF SOUTH CAROLINA PRESS

Published by the University of South Carolina Press
Columbia, South Carolina 29208

www.sc.edu/uscpress

Manufactured in the United States of America

28 27 26 25 24 23 22 21 20 19
10 9 8 7 6 5 4 3 2 1

Library of Congress Cataloging-in-Publication Data
can be found at http://catalog.loc.gov/.

ISBN: 978-1-61117-935-4 (paperback)
ISBN: 978-1-61117-936-1 (ebook)

For Alice, who has waited long enough,
for Tonia, my student and my teacher and
for Helen Fellers, human extraordinaire!

CONTENTS

Chapter One
THEY'RE COMING!
1

Chapter Two
THE MOVIE THAT
ATE MY REC ROOM
5

Chapter Three
THE CREATURE FROM
THE DEEPEST NIGHT!
11

Chapter Four
STORIES OF THE SKY
15

Chapter Five

WHAT'S FUZZY, PURPLE, AND COMING OUR WAY?
21

Chapter Six

ONE MORE DEFENDER OF THE BLUE PLANET
25

Chapter Seven

READY OR NOT!
31

Chapter Eight

PURPLE SPACESHIPS EVERYWHERE
37

Chapter Nine

IT'S ALL IN THE WAY YOU LOOK AT IT
41

EPILOGUE
SCIENCE IN THE SKY
46

CHAPTER ONE

THEY'RE COMING!

I'm Art Smart, and I'm here to give you a warning. Aliens are coming! Or maybe not. It really depends on who you believe. Some people think they'll look like monsters with big heads and oval eyes. Some think they'll look just like us. Some people think they already live next door, like my neighbor, Mr. Baber.

I don't mean that I think Mr. Baber is an alien. I mean *he* thinks they live among us. He's always sitting on his back porch, reading those articles that you see in the Bi-Lo checkout line. I'm talking about the ones with headlines like "THE GOVERNMENT IS WATCHING YOU THROUGH YOUR SMOKE DETECTOR" or "MAN FORCED TO EAT HIS OWN TOENAILS WITH ICE CREAM." Yesterday he was reading one with a picture of a gray, triangle-headed alien on the front. It said, "Is Your Town Crawling with Aliens in Disguise?"

I asked Mom about the alien article, and she just kept putting groceries in the pantry. She popped her head out to look at me over her glasses. "Art, Mr. Baber is harmless. He just wants to have something exciting to believe in."

"I never said he wasn't," I told her. "I was just wondering about the tabloid articles."

She shrugged. "Some people will believe anything. It's not real."

"I'd like to decide what's real and what's not for myself," I told her.

She stared at me again. "Did you steal my son and replace him with a middle-aged professor?"

I ignored that.

"Mom, do you believe in UFOs and aliens?"

She put a mayonnaise jar into the pantry and turned to face me. "Art, my little genius, I believe that not everything can be explained with logic and reason. If we already knew everything there is to know, life would be pretty boring. But I'm more concerned with the mortgage than with spaceships. Don't you have homework?"

"Did it."

"Then go clean your room."

Like that was gonna happen. Anyway, I don't know about the tabloid articles, but I can tell you about *The Mystery of the Sliding Spaceship*. And you can believe me. I'm Smart: Art Smart, Science Detective.

I use science to solve mysteries. For example, what happened to all those chocolate kisses in the cabinet?

Scientific investigation proved that they didn't just grow legs and walk away. The evidence was right there on my dad's face . . . and his fingers . . . and his shirt. "See, chocolate tends to start melting at ninety degrees," I explained to Dad. "Your body heat is over ninety-eight degrees. When you held the chocolate for more than a few seconds, it got all over you."

Dad says that sometimes I'm too smart for my own good, and his too.

But the mystery of the sliding spaceship was a whole lot more exciting than melting chocolate. The sliding spaceship . . . well, that was global, even, or it could have been.

It all happened like this.

UFO stands for Unidentified
Flying Object. Of course,
that doesn't automat-
ically mean that a
UFO is a space-
ship. It can be
anything in the
sky that scientists
haven't identified.
I'll bet that helium
balloon I lost last week
could be a UFO!

CHAPTER TWO

THE MOVIE THAT ATE MY REC ROOM

My best friends, Robbie and Jason, and my cousin, Amy, came to my house to spend the night. Amy is also my best friend, but she was my cousin first. Sometimes, I sleep at their houses too. We play games, watch movies, and eat popcorn and jelly beans until our stomachs are bulging. We stay up late telling scary stories.

My sister, Lisa, was there too, but Mom told her to stay out of our way. She's three years older than me, but not nearly as smart . . . well, okay, she's smart, but I'm smarter. "This is Art's night," Mom told her. "Let him have fun with his friends." Staying out of the way isn't really a problem with Lisa. Except for Amy, who's her cousin too, she can't stand hanging out with my friends and me.

"Why in the world would I want to hang out with you?" she groaned at me. "You're a bunch of science nerds."

"Better than being a drama geek." I told her.

According to Lisa, television is a poor, distant cousin to what she calls "real theatre." She's talking about live acting on stage. She and her friends in the thespian society at school can't get enough of Shakespeare. And last week I caught her singing the Schuyler Sister song from *Hamilton* into her hairbrush. She knows every word by heart. One day, she plans to live in Manhattan and direct on Broadway. But New York is a long way from the upstate of South Carolina. In her words, "You have to have your dreams!" I agree.

Anyway, Lisa stayed in her room at first. I figured she was organizing her costume stash or practicing a monologue or something. Jason, Robbie, Amy, and I played basketball and watched *Aliens from the Purple Planet.* The aliens were creepy and had faces the color of old grape jelly. Worse than that, when they spoke they used wavelengths to take over your brain and made you do stuff like bark like a dog or eat beets for dessert. They could even make you help them take over the world. It was gross. In the end, the people in the town beat the invaders by exposing them to old-school country music. You know, all that cheating, crying, jail-time, kind of stuff. Apparently, the sound waves melted their alien brains. Not too surprising. All that whining melts my brain too. Mom said the movie was cheesy and ridiculous. I agree. There was nothing realistic about it, but it was fun. That's the cool thing about having a scientific brain. You can have an imagination and a sense of humor too. I mean, without imagination, we wouldn't have computers or toys that make fart noises.

When the movie ended, Robbie and Jason started glancing out the windows every few seconds. By then it was dark, and you could barely even make out the trees in the yard. You can see Paris Mountain from our rec room, but at night it just looks like an elephant lying on its stomach. I'm not sure what they were expecting to see.

"Do you think it could really happen?" Robbie mumbled through a mouthful of popcorn. It came out sounding like "D'ya tin illy appen?" but I knew what he meant because I speak fluent Robbie.

"Seriously?" I asked. "Purple aliens?"

"Yeah," Jason nodded. "It could happen. You don't know what's out there."

Amy rolled her eyes. "Both of you are so lame!"

But Jason was right. Scientists had not found any other life in our solar system, but beyond that . . . who knows? It would be pretty self-centered to think we were the only living things in the whole universe. "They'd have to be able to travel a long way to get here," I told them. "If they could come this far they'd have to be really advanced, and I doubt they'd be interested in making us bark like dogs, so . . ."

That's when my door flew open and the lights went out!

Sometimes science fiction can become real science. In 1870 Jules Verne wrote about a submarine in *Twenty Thousand Leagues under the Sea.* Captain Nemo's submarine, the *Nautilus,* contained a lot of features that were unheard of in that time. Now they are common on subs. The communicator devices in the 1960s TV show *Star Trek* were a lot like our cell phones are now. Scientists are already working on teleporters. Wouldn't it be cool to "beam over" to Grandma's for macaroni and cheese?

CHAPTER THREE

THE CREATURE FROM THE DEEPEST NIGHT!

Robbie screamed, and Jason grabbed my arm. There in the doorway was the scariest thing I'd ever seen. Its head was covered with a shiny hood, and its face was glowing green. It had enormous eyes and huge teeth!

"Aaaaaaak!" it screeched.

Robbie made tracks toward the corner, and Jason hit the floor. Even Amy hid behind the couch, but I thought maybe I heard her giggling.

I just stood there. I knew that *Aaaaaaak*. "That's not funny, Lisa!"

Lisa thought it was pretty hilarious, though. After she stopped laughing, she turned on the lights and flipped off the flashlight she was holding under her chin. Then she pulled her silver raincoat hood off her head. "You guys are such big goofs." It sounded funny coming from the alien mask she was wearing, so she pulled it off too.

Amy, Jason, and Robbie were still a little shaky even if they tried to pretend they weren't. But not me. I'm Art Smart, Science Detective. Nothing scares me. Well, not for long anyway . . . except for broccoli. It's all green and looks like a miniature tree. Yuck. My personal feeling on broccoli is that only kids with a vitamin deficiency should be required to eat it. Or maybe they should just dry it and use all of it for firewood. The kids with vitamin deficiencies can just take a chewable vitamin.

"Didn't mom tell you to stay out of here?"

She grinned. "Yeah, but I thought you might need a visit from your friendly neighborhood alien. Besides, I got bored. Is the movie over?"

"Yeah," Jason told her, plopping back down on the couch. "Do you believe in aliens, Lisa?" For some reason, my friends think that just because Lisa is older, her opinion must count for something.

"Only the one that lives in the room next to mine," she laughed.

"Hey," Robbie noted like a true genius, "that's Art's room! Oh!"

Robbie's a little slow to catch on sometimes but he's usually there with the rest of us in the end.

Lisa just smiled. "I suppose anything's possible, but I wouldn't bet on it. Besides, why would they bother with a tiny state like South Carolina when they could see New York City or Los Angeles?"

Sometimes I don't think Lisa appreciates how amazing it is to live here, but I decided not to argue the point.

"I'm making peanut butter and jelly sandwiches," she went on. "Want some?"

"Sure!" I told her. There are times when I like my sister. "Thanks. Will you bring them outside? It's getting hot in here."

"Afraid you might find an alien under the couch?" she asked. "Maybe a spaceship in the closet?"

I ignored that.

Lisa brought some sandwiches to us on the porch and went back inside. She's okay when she's not being the big sister overlord. After that stunt she pulled, I never really thought I'd be glad to see her later, but I was.

It's not too likely that you're going to find an alien under your couch. But scientists have been sending messages out across the universe for a long time. The *Voyager* spacecraft was sent into space in 1977 with recorded messages of welcome in 55 languages. It also had images and sounds from Earth. They hoped that extraterrestrials might find the spacecraft as it traveled through space.

CHAPTER FOUR

STORIES OF THE SKY

Robbie had a new book on astronomy. While we ate, we sat on the back porch to look at the stars. We picked out constellations, pictures in the stars. The really cool thing about constellations is that there's usually an old Greek or Roman myth that goes with each one. People in ancient Greece and Rome used to make up stories to match the stars.

My favorite is the one about Draco, the dragon. This guy named Cadmus (what kind of name is Cadmus?) fought the dragon and won. He planted the dragon's teeth in the ground. The teeth grew into warriors who fought each other until only five were left. Those five helped Cadmus start the city of Thebes.

Amy's favorite is about Perseus, the brave warrior who saved Princess Andromeda from Cetus the sea monster!

"Cool!" Jason yelled. "There's the Big Dipper! The book says they also call that one Ursa Major because it's

supposed to look like a big bear. That's what Ursa Major means, big bear."

I thought it looked more like a dipper than a bear, though.

"Look," Robbie pointed, "There's Orion, the hunter." You can always see Orion by looking for the three stars that make up his belt.

Jason twisted his head. "You made that up. It doesn't look anything like a hunter."

Robbie doesn't like it when somebody says he's making stuff up. He shoved the book at Jason. "It's right here in the book!" He flipped a page. "See! Orion hunted with the goddess Artemis, but he got a little carried away, and a scorpion killed him. Then Zeus put him up in the sky. That's where Scorpio comes from, too." The pictures in the book connected the stars with lines so that Orion really did look like a hunter.

"Well, okay," Jason growled. "I still say he looks more like a couple of trapezoids back to back, but whatever."

"There's Cassiopeia!" I yelled. "She sort of looks like she's sitting in a chair, but it's more like a staircase."

"She's Andromeda's mother," Amy added.

Then we all started finding different shapes and even making up our own stories. It was better than TV. But we got a little loud. Okay, maybe it was more than a *little* loud.

"Quiet down!" yelled our neighbor, Mr. Baber. He's really old and hates loud noise. Sometimes I'm not too crazy about him either.

But my mom made me promise to always be polite to my elders, even grouchy old Mr. Baber. I called, "Yes, sir."

That put an end to our fun. I mean, fun and noise sort of just go together when you're a kid. But then I had a thought.

"Hey," I whispered, "let's look at the moon through the telescope. We can do that without disturbing Mr. Baber."

My grandmother knows I'm a scientific kind of guy, so she gave me this ginormous telescope for my birthday. With it I can see Jupiter and sometimes Saturn. I even saw Pluto once, which used to be a normal planet. But Pluto is so tiny that it got demoted to a dwarf planet. It's almost impossible to see with a backyard telescope. You gotta feel sorry for the little guy.

Before astronomers decided that Pluto was too small to be a planet, people used to memorize the nine planets by saying, "My very educated mother just served us nine pizzas." Every word was a clue so that if you looked at the first letter of each word, you could remember the planet names: Mercury, Venus, Earth, Mars, Jupiter, Saturn, Uranus, Neptune, and Pluto. They call that a mnemonic device. Try saying that three times fast! Now that Pluto got knocked down a notch, my teacher says, "My very educated mother just served us nachos." Okay, I like nachos, so I can live with that, but poor Pluto!

That night, instead of planets, we focused on the moon. The moon goes through stages that depend on how much of the sun is reflected on its surface. In a month's time it can be a full, gibbous, quarter, crescent, or new moon . . . or anything in-between. You would think that a full moon would be great to see through a telescope, but there's too much glare to make out any details. That night, though, it was a few days past the first quarter, perfect for viewing through a telescope. We wanted to look for craters and mountains, but what we saw started all kinds of trouble.

According to NASA, in 2016 astronomer Mike Brown discovered a new planet in our outer solar system. They called it "Planet Nine" . . . really great name, right? Nobody has actually seen it because it's probably about 20 times farther from the sun than Neptune. It might be 10 times the mass of Earth! That's one big planet!

CHAPTER FIVE

WHAT'S FUZZY, PURPLE, AND COMING OUR WAY?

Robbie took a quick breath and stumbled away from the telescope. "Huh?"

Then he just pointed at the telescope and gasped. Sometimes he's such a goof.

Amy took a turn and came away with her mouth open. "Gee!"

Jason looked while I stood there shaking my head at Robbie. "Wow! You've got to see this, Art!"

So I took a peek . . . and then I understood. There was the moon of course, all bright and covered with cool shadows. Then I saw it, just to the lower right of the moon. It was really fuzzy, but it had to be . . . a spaceship! It looked like it was coming right at us.

I gawked at Amy, Robbie, and Jason and they gawked at me. "Aliens from the Purple Planet!" we all yelled.

"I told you kids to quiet down," called our neighbor, Mr. Baber.

"Sorry, Mr. Baber." We all said it at the same time. It sounded like we were practicing for a concert.

We had to do something. "Mom! Dad! There's a spaceship!" I yelled, running inside as fast as I could.

Mom rubbed her nose with the back of her hand and stared at Dad. "I told you not to let them watch that movie."

"Really, Mrs. Smart! We saw it in the telescope!" Robbie almost fell on top of me getting in the door.

Jason did fall, right on his elbows, which is nothing new. That kid hasn't had un-scraped elbows in three months.

"Uncle David, Aunt Sophia, it's for real!" Amy yelled.

"It was purple!" said Jason, "and fuzzy!"

"A furry, purple spaceship?" Mom covered her face with her hands. She does that a lot when she's talking to me.

"Fuzzy," I told her, "not furry. It's like it won't come into focus."

Mom lowered her hand and cleared her throat. "Art, if you're going to lose it whenever you watch a sci-fi movie . . ."

"Oh, come on," Dad laughed and nudged Mom, "I used to watch movies like that all the time. They're just using their imagination. It's good for them."

Then Dad went back to the paper and Mom to her novel.

We made tracks toward the garage, but Lisa was standing there, blocking the way. She planted her size-eight foot in the doorway and stopped us. Do I even need to tell you that Jason couldn't manage to stay in a standing position? This time he went skidding and sat down hard on his rear end. That part of him probably has plenty of bruises too.

"So," my sister laughed with a tip of her head, "what's all the excitement about, nerd herd?"

On June 20, 1969, kids all over America gathered around televisions to watch the very first manned moon landing. Astronauts Neil Armstrong, Michael Collins, and Buzz Aldrin made history that day. Armstrong and Aldrin piloted the lunar module, called the *Eagle,* onto the moon's surface. Neil Armstrong stepped onto the moon's surface and announced, "That's one small step for [a] man, one giant leap for mankind." Maybe one day, I'll pilot a mission to Neptune or beyond. I figure a telescope on my back porch with starry skies overhead is a great place to start.

CHAPTER SIX
ONE MORE DEFENDER OF THE BLUE PLANET

"Lisa, why don't you go back to your cave and leave us alone? This is important," I said, trying to shove my sister out of the way. Unfortunately, she's three inches taller than me and ten pounds heavier.

"Important, huh?" She grinned an evil grin. I swear that girl has a real dark side. "How important? Is it important enough for you to pay for the privilege to pass by?"

"Lisa!" I gritted my teeth. This was embarrassing, but my friends had seen it before. Besides, Jason has a big sister and a big brother. That's one of the reasons he spends so much time face down on the ground. "Lisa, you know I don't have any money." That wasn't quite true. I had five dollars left over from cutting the grass, but I was saving that for a chemistry set I'd found online. I was gonna make a stink bomb. "Look, we saw something really scary through the telescope. Mom and Dad think we're imagining it."

Lisa's expression didn't change much but her voice became a little higher pitched. She pinned Amy with a glare. I guess she expects more from her because she's a girl. "Are these clowns serious?" Then she stared at all of us. "What exactly is scary enough to frighten a bunch of science nerds?"

I decided that shock value might go a long way in this case. "Aliens."

"Oh, come on!" she balked. "You're just freaking out because you were scared by the stupid movie."

"No! He's right," Jason said, pulling himself up with the doorframe. "We saw a spaceship in the telescope."

Lisa laughed so hard I thought she might cough up a lung. "Aliens! Did they wave their light sabers at you and promise to beam you up too? Are you going to meet them downtown at the Liberty Bridge?"

"No . . . we just saw the spaceship." Robbie answered. He doesn't quite understand the concept of sarcasm. Mom says I understand it a little too well.

Amy looked at Robbie. "You are so literal."

I groaned. "Lisa, if we show you, will you help us?"

"Maybe," she shrugged. "There's nothing on TV, and Joni's out of town." Joni is Lisa's best friend. They remind me of twin chipmunks when they get together and sing show tunes. Not that I'd say that to Lisa. She'd kick me like a soccer ball.

"Come on," I told her, and we all ran to the back porch.

I checked the telescope. Yup, it was still there, just to the right of the moon. "Look, but don't move the telescope. I don't want to lose the position.

Lisa smirked at me and then put her eye up to the eyepiece. I could tell by her expression, the second she spotted it. Lisa's mouth flew open, and she slowly pulled away. "You're serious."

We all nodded like four bobble-head dolls in the back window of a Honda.

"Okay then," she said, sounding a little like she'd just been hit in the head with a bag of rocks, "what do we do now?

ART ADDS

I really am saving my money for a chemistry set, but I plan to do more than make stink bombs. I might grow crystals or make some homemade slime to share with Lisa! Did you know that chemists are responsible for understanding the structure of atoms and for the vaccine that helped get rid of smallpox? Also, a chemist named Alexander Fleming discovered penicillin growing in a petri dish by accident. He almost threw the petri dish away before he saw that the mold growing there had killed some bacteria. Some accidents are really lucky!

CHAPTER SEVEN

READY OR NOT!

In the garage, I grabbed up two old football helmets, my new batter's helmet, and two bike helmets. "We might need these!" I told the others

We had to make plans. What did they want? Did they want to share a cure for poison oak or take over the planet? If they were just making friends, great! But, if they attacked, we had to find a way to defend ourselves.

Robbie's eyes got big. "What if they use their hypnotic voices to turn our brains to mush and make us do line dances until our feet drop off?" We all turned to stare at him. Robbie is so strange.

"Maybe we could just play old-style country music, like in the movie." Jason chimed in.

Lisa's mouth dropped open, and she laughed. "Did somebody drop you on your head when you were a baby?"

I was a bit more diplomatic. "That's just a movie. We have to find a real solution. Maybe we can talk to them. They might be reasonable."

"Maybe," Robbie said, "but what if they don't understand our language?"

"I'll bet they have automatic translators!" Jason beamed.

"Okay, maybe they do," Robbie answered, "but what if they're mean and scary like the aliens in the movie, and they don't care what we have to say?"

"He's right." Amy agreed. "We have to be ready just in case."

Just in case they did have hypnotic voices, we shoved peanut butter in our ears. Okay, I know how weird that sounds, but have you ever tried to hear anything with peanut butter in your ears? It works better than cotton.

We decided to make the garage our base. It was defensible because there was only one opening if you didn't count the windows. We could make the garage door go up and down and maybe crush an alien if we had to.

We tested it out. Jason stood outside the door and ran toward it like he was gonna rush in. Unfortunately, Robbie had left his skateboard in the driveway, and, just as I was lowering the door, Jason tripped and went sliding feet first. He looked like a clown at the circus. He landed half in, half out of the garage, with the door on his chest. Luckily, the door stops automatically when it hits something, so Jason was okay, but he sure was mad. "GET THIS THING OFF OF ME!" We decided just to watch through the windows—the garage door was too dangerous.

We packed up cans of Vienna sausages, jars of peanut butter, boxes of crackers, and bottles of orange drink. It's important to have food supplies when you might need to go into battle. Plus, if the aliens were friendly, we could offer them a snack!

We put shields on the windows. Okay, they were just cardboard with peepholes, but what else do you expect on short notice?

We covered our helmets with aluminum foil for extra protection. We thought that might help stop those hypnotic brain waves from getting through. Lisa shook her head. "MOM'S NOT GONNA LIKE THE FACT THAT WE USED UP ALL OF HER FOIL," she warned, "BUT IT IS FOR A GOOD CAUSE." We could barely understand her through the peanut butter.

I got the first-aid kit out of the car in case we needed a bandage or alcohol wipes. It pays to be ready.

The last thing we did was call the police department. We decided to call the non-emergency number because it wasn't really an emergency . . . yet. We had to clean the peanut butter out of one ear to hear. When the

operator answered, I put her on speaker so everybody could hear, and explained that we'd seen a spaceship in the telescope. We just wanted to let somebody know in case they land. I thought I heard somebody laughing on the other end.

"Um . . . can I get your name and address please?" she asked.

"Sure, Art Smart, 353 Poinsett Avenue, Greenville, South Carolina," I told her.

"Mr. Smart, how old are you?"

"Ten."

"Have you mentioned this to your parents?"

"Yes, but they don't think it's real."

"Alright. We'll have a car in that area soon. I'll try to have him stop by. You understand, of course, that unless you have an emergency, I can't promise anything."

"Yes, ma'am." I ended the call.

"Did you hear laughing?" Amy asked, but nobody answered.

We replaced the peanut butter, and we went back to the porch to check the telescope. Big mistake!

Devices that translate one language into another actually exist. That's right, I could tell Mr. Baber in English how sorry I was for interrupting his quiet time, and he could hear it in French. Not that he would understand it or believe it!

CHAPTER EIGHT

PURPLE SPACESHIPS EVERYWHERE

I was the first to look. The ship was still there, but it didn't look any closer. That was a relief. Maybe they were just hanging out, observing. Maybe they weren't planning to do anything except observe us.

Then Jason tripped over Robbie's foot and smack . . . into the telescope. It twisted and wobbled. For a second I thought I was about to have a bunch of glass shards instead of a telescope lens. But it didn't fall, thank goodness.

I picked Jason up. He wiped off his hands. "SORRY, DUDE!"

"NO HARM DONE!" I yelled back. Then I looked into the eyepiece. This time, instead of the moon, I could see Venus. It's the easiest planet to find because it's the brightest. And just to the lower right of Venus was the purple spaceship. It had slid all the way over to Venus that quickly. "Boy! That was fast!"

"WHAT?" They all asked. We had to yell to hear each other through the peanut butter in our ears. I'm sure that didn't make our neighbor, Mr. Baber, too happy.

"The spaceship!" I yelled. "It moved, just like that!" I snapped my fingers.

"Let me see." Jason grabbed at the optical tube of the telescope. His hand slipped and it moved a whole foot to the right.

"Oh great!" Robbie yelled. "Now we've lost the aliens for sure."

I looked back into the eyepiece, adjusted the tube, and focused, this time on Saturn. It's pretty easy to find with a telescope. It's huge and has bands of clouds. Okay, but here's the mystery, the spaceship was right there, just southeast of Saturn. "It moved again!" I yelled. Something was definitely off.

Robbie and Jason both took a look, then Amy, but no matter where they looked in the night sky, there was the spaceship. "The aliens know we're onto them. They've zeroed in on the telescope, and now they're following us!" Robbie called.

We were all getting a little bit panicky.

"Run!" Jason said with a yelp. "Hide!"

"Let me see!" Lisa shoved them both aside. She moved the telescope all around the sky. "This just doesn't make sense. Even spaceships don't move that fast!"

Jason's eyes grew to the size of baseballs. "Unless there are spaceships all over the sky! There's a whole armada of spaceships!"

Okay, that was even scarier.

Lisa shoved the eyepiece back at me. Everywhere I looked, there was a spaceship. I aimed the lens at Lisa and focused as well as I could. There on her big, puffy-looking, unfocused face, was a purple spaceship. "Wait a minute!" I hollered.

I was beginning to get a really funny feeling about the purple aliens.

ART ADDS

Saturn is the sixth planet from the sun and is made mostly of hydrogen. It's huge, and you can see it even without a telescope. Most of us know it because of its ginormous rings. Those rings are mostly made of chunks of ice and dust! Who knew ice and dust could be so interesting!

CHAPTER NINE

IT'S ALL IN THE WAY YOU LOOK AT IT

Mom stepped onto the porch and almost collided with Jason, who was running for cover. "Whatcha looking at?"

"Huh?" we asked.

Mr. Baber yelled out. "You kids have been screaming all night. Quiet down before I call your parents!" We sure didn't have any trouble hearing him.

My mom turned bright red. "Sorry about that, Mr. Baber."

"Why are all of you yelling so much?" Mom narrowed her eyes at Robbie. Then she got closer to his ear and scrunched up her nose. "What on Earth has gotten into all of you? And Lisa, really!" Mom ran back into the house and they came out and handed us all wet paper towels with dish detergent on them. "Clean the peanut butter out of your ears. It's dangerous . . . and disgusting." All of us looked kind of like we'd been caught drinking milk straight out of the bottle.

Mom watched us clean out the peanut butter and then she put one eye up to the telescope. "Hmmm . . . that's interesting."

"Um, Mom," I began, "maybe I'd better explain."

That's when the doorbell rang. It was like a stampede, the five of us running toward the door with Mom trailing behind. I got there first and did what Mom always said not to do. I opened up the door without asking who was there. But I had a feeling about this one, and Mom wasn't going to like this, considering what I'd just figured out.

I was right. There was a man in a blue police uniform standing there. He stared at the five of us gaping back at him. "Hello, I'm Officer Mathis. I'd like to speak to a Mr. Art Smart."

My mom stared at me like I'd grown horns. "Officer Mathis, this is my son, Art. Would you mind telling me what this is all about?"

"Yes, ma'am, it's only a precaution. We got a call about a spaceship. Things are slow tonight, so I said I'd check it out." He winked at Mom.

The groan that came out of Mom's throat made me think I'd be doing some serious time making this up to her. She might even make me fold laundry. "Why don't you come out onto the porch, officer?" All of us, including Dad, who had joined us, walked out back. "Art was just about to explain. Weren't you, Art?" Her glare would have melted the bars in a prison.

"Mom," I began, when we were all standing there on the porch, "I think I know what's going on, but maybe Dad and Officer Mathis should look at what we've been seeing, first."

They did. "Well, it does sort of look like a spaceship," Dad said.

"A purplish spaceship," Officer Mathis agreed, but he didn't seem to be too alarmed.

"Yeah, that's what we thought," I admitted. "But just now I noticed that whenever you move the telescope, the ship slides to wherever you point the telescope." Mom lifted an eyebrow. Dad groaned. Officer Mathis just grinned. "Of course, that can only mean one thing. Mom," I asked, "do you have any more of those alcohol pads?" Mom actually carries those around. It says something about how messy the people in this house can be and about how much she hates fingerprints on her tablet. She handed me an alcohol wipe.

"I suppose it's possible for the spaceships to be all over the place," I told them, as I unfolded the wipe, "but I doubt they'd always be in the same part of the telescope range, always on the lower right. So it had to be something else. In science we always look for the most logical solution." I reached up and wiped the lens, showing the alcohol pad to everybody else. "In this case, grape jelly."

"Ack!" my sister moaned. "Grape jelly! All this for a blob of grape jelly!"

Robbie and Jason didn't say anything, but I noticed Robbie was wiping his fingers off on his jeans.

"Next time," Mom sighed, "wash your hands before you use the telescope. Officer, can I get you a cup of coffee?"

The Mystery of the Sliding Spaceship was solved because that's what I do. I'm a scientific kind of guy, and I solve mysteries, even if it does take me a few minutes to catch on.

So I don't suppose we'll be having any visits from purple aliens this week, but if they decide to show up, we'll be ready. Because Art Smart, Science Detective, is always ready for anything . . . except broccoli.

There are all kinds of telescopes from backyard telescopes like the one in this story to gamma-ray telescopes. One of the coolest was launched into space in 1990 and still sends back pictures from outer space. It's called the Hubble telescope. It's a reflecting type that orbits the Earth and has helped us to discover how galaxies form and all kinds of other facts about the universe. One day maybe we'll get to see those aliens from the purple planet, but for now I'll stick to stargazing.

Did you know that even though Galileo Galilei is often given credit for inventing the telescope, he was really only the first person to use it for astronomy? A German spectacle-maker named Hans Lipperhey was the first person to patent a telescope on September 25, 1608.

Lipperhey's telescope used a curved lens to magnify objects as big as three times their regular size.

When Galileo read about the telescope he made his own. One of his telescopes could magnify objects as much as thirty times their real size!

To find out more about Galileo and astronomy, try these books:

Galileo for Kids His Life and Ideas,
by Richard/Alrin Panchyk

Galileo the Genius Who Faced the Inquisition,
by Philip Steeler

Starry Messenger: Galileo Galilei,
by Peter Sis

What can you see in the night sky?

Try looking for these constellations and planets. A map of the stars will help. There are even phone apps that show star maps.

Venus is the easiest planet to see, and you can almost always see it without a telescope. Look to the west. It's the brightest planet out there after sunset.

Saturn, Jupiter, Mercury, and Mars can also be seen, but you may need binoculars or a small telescope.

The constellation Orion is simple to find. Just look for the three stars that make up his belt. Then find the two trapezoids that form his tunic.

The Big Dipper looks just like it sounds. Just look northward and you'll see its handle and bowl like a huge pot in the sky. Then look close by to find the Little Dipper.

Cassiopeia is easy to spot because she looks like a set of stairs.

Have fun stargazing.

To read more about constellations and mythology, try these books:

Glow-in-the-Dark Constellations:
A Field Guide for Young Stargazers,
    by C. E. Thompson and Randy Chewning

Zoo in the Sky:
A Book of Animal Constellations,
    by Jacqueline Mitton, Christina Balit,
    and Wil Tirion

Once upon a Starry Night:
A Book of Constellations,
    by Jacqueline Mitton and Christina Balit